I'M SO FINE
A LIST OF FAMOUS MEN
& WHAT I HAD ON

BOOKS BY KHADIJAH QUEEN

Conduit (Akashic Books)
Black Peculiar (Noemi Press)
Fearful Beloved (Argos Books)
Non-Sequitur (Litmus Press)

YESYES BOOKS   PORTLAND

KHADIJAH QUEEN

I'M
SO
FINE

A LIST OF FAMOUS MEN & WHAT I HAD ON

A NARRATIVE

FIRST EDITION, 2017
SECOND PRINTING
ISBN 978-1-936919-46-8

PRINTED IN THE UNITED STATES OF AMERICA

PUBLISHED BY YESYES BOOKS
1614 NE ALBERTA ST
PORTLAND, OR 97211
YESYESBOOKS.COM

KMA SULLIVAN, PUBLISHER
JILL KOLONGOWSKI, MANAGING EDITOR
STEVIE EDWARDS, SENIOR EDITOR, BOOK DEVELOPMENT
ALBAN FISCHER, GRAPHIC DESIGNER
BEYZA OZER, DEPUTY DIRECTOR OF SOCIAL MEDIA
AMBER RAMBHAROSE, CREATIVE DIRECTOR OF SOCIAL MEDIA
PHILLIP B. WILLIAMS, COEDITOR IN CHIEF, *VINYL*
AMIE ZIMMERMAN, EVENT COORDINATOR
JOANN BALINGIT, ASSISTANT EDITOR
MARY CATHERINE CURLEY, ASSISTANT EDITOR
MARK DERKS, ASSISTANT EDITOR
COLE HILDEBRAND, ASSISTANT EDITOR
CARLY SCHWEPPE, ASSISTANT EDITOR, *VINYL*
HARI ZIYAD, ASSISTANT EDITOR, *VINYL*

Damn u, u're so fine

—PRINCE

CONTENTS

MA$E pre-preacher cleared a whole Atlanta dance floor when I showed up / 21

When I met LL Cool J I had just quit Fatburger / 22

Montell Jordan came to the drive-thru / 23

I never met Snoop Dogg but I met his homie Lil' ½ Dead / 24

When I worked in retail my coworker said Suge Knight liked her hairy legs / 25

I never met Donald Trump but I sure have been grabbed by the you-know-what / 26

I never met Bill Cosby but I met Beverly Johnson at Magic Mountain / 27

We met Shai at the Fox Hills Mall / 28

A boy people said was Sammy Davis Jr.'s son went to Beverly at the same time I did / 29

I was nine or ten when I met Minister Louis Farrakhan at Mosque No. 27 on Crenshaw / 30

My dad said he took us to see both Nelson Mandela & Muhammad Ali / 31

Speaking of those pictures / 32

Since Optimus Prime counts so does the KITT car / 33

Josh Duhamel walked past me really fast / 34

Al Pacino is on the short side but very gracious / 35

When we met Tupac we had just left the Arena on Sunset because it was gay night & we couldn't get in / 36

Walter Mosley mostly looked at our cleavage / 38

The Wayans brothers did not look at all / 39

I am from Los Angeles obviously / 40

Comedians can be the best / 41

Edward Norton just stared / 43

Prince called me up onstage at the Pontiac Silverdome / 44

When I met Andre 3000 at the Ralph's in Burbank / 45

I met Keyshawn Johnson on the USC campus in one of the dorm rec rooms / 46

I'M SO FINE
A LIST OF FAMOUS MEN
& WHAT I HAD ON

I MET MARCUS CHONG ON THE 105 BUS METHOD ACTING I was going home in a flowered dress after work I worked at Fatburger I was 18 & I think he was twice that I had my uniform in my backpack with my Statistics homework & *Woman Warrior* I recognized him & said I liked *Panther* (this was way before *The Matrix*) he asked for my number we talked on the phone he came to visit me on his bike since he didn't live far from my job & ordered a veggie burger I had a lemonade on my 15-minute break in my black Fatburger outfit & ugly foodservice shoes he asked me on a date I said yes he called with the plan I said I thought we were going somewhere but he wanted to make me dinner at his house I said No I don't know you well enough to go to your house he got angry The End

I MET CUBA GOODING JR. AT THE BEVERLY CENTER FOOD COURT I was 16
Boyz N the Hood had just come out & my best friend Tiffany dared me to ask if
I could hug him he said I was beautiful & seemed really happy to get that hug
but I brown-blushed nervously & he sat a few booths away with his friend
& veggie slices from Sbarro & smiled a lot I wore Tiff's Kente cloth bomber
jacket & red lipstick I had perfect skin & didn't drink carbonated beverages

are these real experiences
that she had?

THE BEVERLY CENTER FOOD COURT IS ALSO WHERE I MET DEVANTE'S BROTHER FROM JODECI I forgot his name but we didn't really meet he was just looking at my eyes then looking at my ass as I kept walking I really liked red lipstick back then I got it that day with my saved allowance at Rexall across the street a blue-red in a gold case & we both had on white jeans I was 17 & I remember it was summer

DAVE CHAPPELLE ALSO LOOKED AT MY ASS & he also said Daaaaaaaaaaamn we were in the frozen food section at Ralph's in North Hollywood & I half-smiled I was wearing my favorite old Levis with the hole at the left side belt loop & had just moved back to L.A. with my two-year-old

CHRIS ROCK DID THE SAME THING same jeans at the movie theater across from the Beverly Center & he thought he wouldn't be recognized with that newsboy cap on but I saw him he looked twice

DJ QUIK WAS REALLY NICE I was in his video because I did modeling & movie/ TV extra work to pay for school he didn't say or do anything disrespectful & I appreciated that I had on a striped dress fitted & long with a slit on the side I was 19 & needed a ride home I'd let my sister use the car & the shoot ended early so the director let me use his cell one of those bigass Motorola flips but no one was answering at home so I had to call this Nigerian guy that I had just met the day before & he kind of creeped me out but the set was in the straight hood & it was getting dark so I called him for a ride he came zooming up the street 15 minutes later in a red BMW & wanted to hang out but I really really didn't we were going to the Century Club later me & my girls so I said we would meet him there but I really wasn't going to meet him he could just find me if he could & if he didn't oh well & we went it was fun at first my sister's friend had DDs & never wore underwear so we got in free everywhere & we saw a bunch of Lakers then she had to go & get drunk we had to save her from this boxer dude who was trying to take her home she didn't know what the f she was doing so I stayed with her while our younger sisters went to get the car then the guy grabbed her by the arm I could see it turning red I wouldn't let go of her hand I called for help no one came my shoe fell off where the fuck are they with the got damn car I thought & called for help again louder over & over & finally finally a bouncer came & told the guy to leave & the boxer guy looked at me & acted like he was going to walk off then turned around & lunged I thought he was going to punch me in the face but I didn't move I didn't flinch because fuck him but thank God the bouncer held him back even though he rolled his eyes at us once the boxer finally left & mumbled something about stupid bitches

RIGHT AFTER *JASON'S LYRIC* CAME OUT MY SISTER & I SAW BOKEEM
WOODBINE AT THE FOOTLOCKER we looked but he didn't want to be seen
he walked in with a really skinny woman with straight black hair to her knees
& white shorts & a racer-back tank top she tried on a bunch of sneakers &
didn't want any of them so they left kind of together he seemed irritated
& didn't hold the door open for her I had on my white Guess T-shirt with
the gold letters tucked into high-waisted ankle-zipped acid-washed jeans &
I thought I was fly

whats the importance of not only
her clothing but other people's
that she remembers?

Is it just her during?

are these chronological?

WE DIDN'T MEET HIM BUT WE SURE DID SEE MORRIS CHESTNUT in the
Beverly Center he was way shorter & way finer than we thought & he walked
really fast after he got off the escalator unzipping his jacket I was too stunned
to speak anyway I mean allofthatchocolate & the goatee was on poiiiiiint so
all me & Tiff could do was try to keep our squeals in until he had passed us all
the way I had on a black velvet bodysuit & black jeans my corkscrew curls in
an updo just another ditch day 11th grade

(handwritten margin note, rotated:) HS almost like things like talking, esp w/

OHMYGOD BUT WHEN WE SAW DEVANTE ON THE ESCALATOR with his arms bandaged to cover fresh tattoos everybody freaked out screaming except me & of course I thought his green eyes were amazing & of course I knew all the words to all the Jodeci songs but I'm on the quiet side & not really one to be jostling in a crowd there were six of us that day ditching science because the teacher was a perv on top of being boring I stayed at the lower level with our backpacks while everyone else got autographs but no hugs due to the tatt situation I had on a sundress white with blue flowers & some brown clogs it was picnic day for our crew & we all dressed alike that day it was clogs & flowered dresses &/all the cheerleaders hated us because the football players started to sit with us at lunch)

ONE DAY TIFF WAS SAD BECAUSE IT WAS THE TENTH ANNIVERSARY OF
HER MOTHER'S DEATH & SHE JUST REALLY WANTED TO GO SEE MICHAEL
JACKSON she said she knew where the family lived in Encino because her
sister used to babysit Tito's kids so we left school after the first bell & got
on the bus with just enough fare we thought & rode three different buses &
walked a bunch of suburban blocks it was like 90 degrees & I had on jeans
& socks & sneakers & a crop top HOTASFUCK carrying my backpack when
we finally got there no one was home & we looked at the pool on the other
side of the lattice gate with deeper longing than our previous desire to see MJ
although I don't think I need to explain how much we stayed loving Michael
Jackson or how the day he died was the day before my sister's wedding in St.
Lucia & Tiffany arrived at the hotel weeping but I might have to explain how
much I had already walked for him when I was a kid I braved a full mile to
the house of a neighbor I hated just to listen to *Thriller* because they were the
only ones in the neighborhood with a record player my mother broke mine
just because my father had bought it & tore my favorite posters in half the one
where he had on the yellow sweater & the one with the Jackson 5 all smiling
& sequins & pre too much surgery but somehow I protected the record so I
would ignore the alcoholics playing spades at the kitchen table & swat the
hands of the boy trying to lift my skirt & I would sit on the neighbor's smoke-
blue fabric couch listening to MJ flattening my lap with Black magazines &
anyway no answer at the Jackson compound so we walked all the way back to
the bus stop there was a Burger King next to it with AC so we took a chance
& used part of our return fare to get Whopper Jrs & $0.15 cups of ice water
we were so hungry & thirsty by then & there was a payphone in the parking
lot so after we ate & drank we called my dad for a ride we called a bunch of
times hanging up before the answering machine came on so we could use the

same quarter but he never answered we were stuck & freaking out a little bit we ended up asking random strangers for change the first few people gave us nickels & quarters & dimes but one guy gave us a $5 bill because he said he had daughters & it wasn't safe for us to ask strangers for money he also offered us a ride but we said no thank you because he could've been a perv & this was years before some kids accused MJ of making them drink Jesus juice & even then to believe white people over MJ seemed like betrayal like here they go trying to take everything from us again our geniuses our heroes our talents our loves & if it's true it hurts it hurts it hurts & anyway the bus came & we got back to school in time for 6th period

11

MY SISTER & I MET KEANU REEVES AT OUR HIGH SCHOOL he rode up on a black motorcycle & when he took off his helmet I thought my sister would faint we were in the P.E. office by the basketball court doing stat girl duties for the team & I told her to look out of the window & this boy who liked her immediately got jealous that fool rushed outside puffing up his chest & trying to act all hard when Keanu joined the guys on the court for a pickup game but Keanu was so cool about it & when the game was over I dragged my suddenly shy sister out there I thought her face would explode she turned so red & smiled so hard & she couldn't talk I had to be the one to ask Keanu if I could take a pic of them together luckily we happened to have a disposable camera that day & my sister who had a foot-thick scrapbook of Keanu clippings from *YM* & *Details* & *People* got her own picture to put on the front she had on my clothes that day a jewel-toned striped blazer & everything else black velvet choker bodysuit stirrups & suede platform sandals plus her own burgundy wool beret Keanu had a patchy beard & his hair reached his shoulders he wore basketball shorts & a faded black shirt with a tiny hole at the neck & smiled

seems real?

I DON'T REMEMBER HOW OLD I WAS WHEN I SAW LOU RAWLS but we were on Wilshire somewhere with my mom & he drove a Rolls the color of rich cream every finger had gold & diamonds on it & the woman passenger wore a white fur coat & her bouffant stretched high enough to almost brush the inside roof of the car she also had on a lot of jewelry but not as much as Lou & we knew who he was because he had just performed on *Solid Gold* or *Soul Train* & I must have had on a dress or skirt because I remember my legs were cold & my mom said for us to wave so we waved & he smiled & tapped the horn & glided on down the street in sparse traffic

MY MOM WAS WAITING AT THE BUS STOP IN 1960 WHEN SHE SAW
CHUCK CONNORS he flirted with her did a double take as she waited to ride
the Western line down Hollywood Boulevard to her job at Max Factor she
was only 21 & had just moved to L.A. & still wore crinoline under her dresses
he drove by the next day too in a long white Cadillac convertible with cattle
horns Texas-ing the hood & his face all sideburns & grin she said it was fun
watching him try but I didn't give him no play

MY MOM MET LAYZIE BONE FROM BONE THUGS-N-HARMONY AT THE
AIRPORT she saw his cornrows & the way he was dressed & asked if he was a
rapper when he said yes she said May I have your autograph for my daughters
I don't know what happened to that page of her address book that he signed
on a slant but I had on cutoff sweatpants & a holey *Purple Rain* t-shirt when
she showed it to me & I remember I was reading *Sula* on the couch

MY MOM HAS NEVER BEEN VERY STARSTRUCK BUT SHE LOVED HER SOME BILLY DEE my sister & I loved *Star Wars* & when she saw Billy Dee Williams smiling at her from a 3x5 trading card we got from the Circle K she went a little nuts hollering & snatching at who we thought of as Lando Calrissian she shouted Whoa! Oh! & snatched it & smiled & said May I have that one to put in my wallet pleeeeease my mother has a gorgeous smile & I liked Lando too but not THAT much so I said sure & giggled & I must have been 4 or 5 when *Star Wars* came out & probably had on a Kmart short set & when she ran into him at the Whole Foods in Studio City in 2004 she said to herself(OHMYGODMYHAIR ISNOTRIGHT MYCLOTHES ARENOTRIGHT MYSHOES ARENOTRIGHT)& hid behind a pyramid of assorted vitamins

SO MAYBE SHE WAS A LITTLE STARSTRUCK ESPECIALLY IN THE EARLY MOTOWN ERA she & her sister Valerie made their way from Inkster to the front row at the 20 Grand in Detroit to see David Ruffin & they made the biggest noise in the place so of course he noticed them he asked their names & sang to them as he took their hands & a bunch of the other women in the audience fell on the floor in a faint my mother thought he was so cool it was 1955 & she was in her last year of high school & had on a gold lamé dress her Aunt Mittie had given her

A FEW WEEKS LATER SHE SAW HARRY BELAFONTE WALKING DOWN THE
STREET she & her cousin Flavis Davis & sister Evelyn strolled to a show at
the Fisher Theater walking down Woodward all of them wore kitten heels &
pillbox hats & white gloves & chiffon & organdy dresses & full makeup they
used torn paper bag strips the night before to twist their hair into tight curls
they called croconos & Flavis noticed the man ahead of them in an avocado-
colored suit jacket & whispered *is that Harry Belafonte* so they sped up & got
close enough to him that he said hello & smiled before he turned the corner &
then they saw Eartha Kitt with a little white dog on a leash she was sprinting
across the street to the Fisher wearing a white capelet & my mother said I've
got to have one of those for myself the cape not the dog

MY DAD PLAYED A PEDESTRIAN IN THE MOVIE MR. & MRS. SMITH he is retired & to relieve his boredom one day when we were talking on the phone I suggested he work as an extra like I did way back when & he thought it was a great idea he loves movies so he got headshots done & since he looks a little bit Middle Eastern he got plenty of work he would take a bunch of newspapers or a book to set probably something by Tom Wolfe or Cornel West to read between takes & impress people & he said Angelina Jolie (who my toddler son was crushing on I mean we couldn't turn the page of a magazine if she was in it in that silver *Tomb Raider* outfit he would put his whole hand on the page & say *it's HER mommy*) is down to earth & Brad Pitt is the nicest guy much nicer than that *Zoolander* guy who instructed the AD to tell the extras not to make eye contact & I'm not sure what I wore or if it's really relevant but generally when I talk on the phone I have on yoga pants & an old T-shirt like the one my Auntie Betty sent me from her favorite Vegas casino

THE SAME YEAR I FOUND OUT WHO AUDIE MURPHY WAS I GOT STRETCH MARKS I was 12 & living in a battered women's shelter in Long Beach with my mother & sister & noticed the light striations after my first shower there I was filling out too fast & eating too much junk food I put on sandals & a loose pale blue summer dress that tied at the shoulders & saw the woman in the bunk across the room organizing pictures in a raggedy green photo album she lay there propped up on a thin elbow looking at Audie Murphy so hard her inch-thick glasses fogged up & chattered to herself about his movies I think it bothered her son who was my age & very smart but he didn't complain he took really good care of her she would kiss the pictures & say in a clear voice I might be tall & you might be short Audie Murphy but you'd better tell those Western girls you're all mine

MA$E PRE-PREACHER CLEARED A WHOLE ATLANTA DANCE FLOOR WHEN
I SHOWED UP I was on leave visiting my cousin Keke & didn't even know
what was happening until everyone was pushed to walk along the wall the
only lights a low & garish yellow against the dark walls & just as it seemed
the dance floor had emptied a rough hand touched mine & MA$E walked up
to me & said Why you mad at me I thought that was kind of silly so I said
I'm not mad at you honey I was in really good shape two years into military
service & showed off in a white crop top black silk pants & pearl choker I had
my curls all tight with AmPro & right now I am laughing at myself

"voice in me head"

WHEN I MET LL COOL J I HAD JUST QUIT FATBURGER it was a Saturday morning & without knowing how I would afford to pay for it I drove my new-used powder blue 1988 Oldsmobile Cutlass Supreme with my sister to the Sam Goody's off Washington Blvd & we met our friend/ex-coworker Squeak AKA Slim she wore rimless glasses & was 6 feet tall & nicknamed by the same ex-coworker who nicknamed me Twin 1 & my younger sister Twin 2 because she couldn't pronounce our names but our boss Lena could she called our names all damn day she had a slight goatee & crooked glasses & a limp she was mean & because she said we thought we were cute she loved making us do the dirtiest work like clean the toilets & underneath the grill especially when the general manager changed our title to customer service rep & we were supposed to engage the guests not deal with food or cleaning so much & one day she spilled something on the floor & told me to mop it up right now this was after she accused me of stealing $20 from the register so I was already mad & Mike the grill guy said she found it under the counter the next morning so I looked her right in the sweaty face & said you clean it up & dropped the mop like a microphone & walked out to applause anyway fast forward the three of us stood together in line to buy LL's new CD talking shit about Lena's missing side teeth I had on black slacks & black Aerosole sandals & a cheap silky-polyester Rampage button-down with cap sleeves & graphic blue sunflowers & carried my lipstick & wallet in a tiny pleather backpack I'm sure I looked a hot poor mess but oh well we got to see LL lick them lips & smile & sign our posters & CDs I sent the poster to my niece in Michigan & the CD wasn't all that good but I did like that one song with Boyz II Men we bumped that in the Oldsmo & I still miss that car's hellified bass

the details in this one are perfect to make you feel like you're there

22

MONTELL JORDAN CAME TO THE DRIVE-THRU as I was clocking out the day before I quit so I went outside to get his autograph for one of my nieces who thought he was soooooo fine he was in a black Suburban with 50-11 dudes & was really cool about it & didn't try to hit on me I probably smelled like Fat Fries even though I'd changed out of my uniform & into khaki shorts he turned the music way down to hear me better & seemed really tired I knew that feeling I still had to take two buses home & get up at 5:30 the next morning to make it to 8am statistics class in Santa Monica & try not to get flashed like earlier that day by a barefoot homeless man in a filthy cloth diaper-thing I was too tired to be anything but mad that I had to stop studying & leave my seat on the bus bench as he swung his pale penis around like a stripper tassel I screamed get the hell out of my face! & he sagged like an empty burlap sack & walked away revealing the thong quality of the diaper which made me throw up in my mouth a little bit & a cop strolled out of the nearby Winchell's sipping a large cup of coffee & asked if I was all right he said do you want me to arrest him I said no I just want to keep reading *The Salt Eaters*

\? wnats anis

23

I NEVER MET SNOOP DOGG BUT I MET HIS HOMIE LIL' ½ DEAD it was a video shoot for ½ Dead that I don't think ever came out another extra assignment my sister & I were both chosen for & paid a premium on top of the non-union rate but it was not enough for what we had to go through the dozen of us girls there had no dressing room so we packed the tiny ladies' room four at a time to change into wardrobe as ½ Dead's degenerate entourage kept knocking on the door & trying to peek underneath & making lewd comments ½ Dead himself flashed cash stacks at me & got mad when I refused his proposal to kick it later all of a sudden I was a stuck-up bitch & then it was time to start the shoot we got called to set & the smoke machine was going on the faux dance floor & midway through the unremarkable song one of the goons tried to pull my sister's dress down in the front his finger actually touching her chest the AD had no control & ½ Dead who looked half-dead I mean it was like his whole aura was dirty he got on his bitch tirade again until one of the girls started grinding on him & pulling her skirt up revealing a thong & the entourage went crazy throwing dollars at her my sister & I put on our sneakers with our dresses & got our stuff & our signed vouchers because they damn sure were gonna pay us regardless because that shit was over the fucking top & we couldn't get out of there fast enough we started hearing threats

WHEN I WORKED IN RETAIL MY COWORKER SAID SUGE KNIGHT LIKED HER HAIRY LEGS & I don't know how true it was but she said he bought the gold chain she wore every day & this was the year Tupac died & I drove my Oldsmo with the lights on in the daytime she & I were both 19 & had to wear skirt suits or slacks in our department we sold CD players & handheld recorders & tried to get people to buy warranties & she could talk those customers into buying almost anything & she tried to help me think beyond thrifting & Wet Seal she tried to tell me about Girbaud jeans & Gucci bags & she really loved her small Chanel I don't remember her name but I remember a dude who worked in the AV department who kept trying to add me on LinkedIn 20 years after the fact like for real nope & I won't say if my coworker got hurt but she made a fact out of fear & once I remember makeup over bruises the 1990s dangerous for women like any other decade like now & the main thing about the guy trying to add me on LinkedIn is how close he stood to me whenever I wore my mother's baby blue v-neck button down because he was trying to look down the front

I NEVER MET DONALD TRUMP BUT I SURE HAVE BEEN GRABBED BY THE YOU-KNOW-WHAT & I really don't even want his name in my book & I almost didn't tell this story but sometimes it's important to name names & the luxury of fame is that it doesn't matter what a nobody says if you have enough money you can buy any kind of truth you want when you're a star they let you do it & actually when you're a man in general the one who did that to me wasn't anyone famous it was a homeless man on the La Brea bus I was 15 & had on a white T-shirt & a denim skirt I was with my mother & she tried to protect me but he chased me from the front of the bus to the back & the driver who happened to be really tall & muscular with his uniform sleeves rolled up past his biceps & sunglasses on with a strap he had to stop the bus at Rodeo by the old movie theater & push the homeless guy down the exit stairs & even on the street he still kept banging on the flimsy doors & sticking out his tongue & shouting

"I never met X but I met Y "
why name the first name?

I NEVER MET BILL COSBY BUT I MET BEVERLY JOHNSON AT MAGIC MOUNTAIN with my dad & my sister one summer in the mid-1980s & she had on an oversized cardigan & jeans casual but lovely my dad chatted her up while we rode the Colossus with her daughter he said he asked for her number & she politely declined I remember her grace & regality & lace-up boots she sat on the bench with her feet crossed at the ankle so when she went public about Cosby drugging & trying to assault her I immediately believed her & not him I have seen enough of powerful men by now to know she had nothing to gain by going public & the truth of beauty means both spotlights & shadows find you & it takes more than instinct to know where to stand on the stage & I don't mean looks all the time I mean all women are all beautiful & I wish we knew it in ways that make us realize the relative insignificance of the arrangement of external features so we might as well not get so caught up & my dad had a lot of nerve right I mean some men have a lot of damn nerve in general & I think my sister & I had on matching Hawaiian shirts that day & wore them tucked in I didn't wear that shirt again & not long after that I fell in love with fashion & asked my dad to start buying me issues of *Vogue*

what does this mean?

We met Shai at the Fox Hills Mall I remember because we were trying on clothes & trying to convince one of our friends not to shoplift a lace push-up bra & panty set she had a date that night with her crush & no cute underwear we said *Girrrrl you better keep your clothes on* & who walked in the store but the tall cute one with the curly hair she forgot all about her date & her draws because she loooooooved Shai especially the tall cute one with the curly hair she got dressed & got a hug & an autograph I probably had on one of my dad's old BOSS sweatshirts that shrank in the dryer because I didn't have many clothes I was 16 & that was the year our house burned down & I left Beverly Hills High where my fashion technology teacher presented *Gone With the Wind* as a good example of costume design so I requested to be excused to the library where I read *The Autobiography of Malcolm X* until the class finished watching all 238 minutes of that shit

A BOY PEOPLE SAID WAS SAMMY DAVIS JR.'S SON WENT TO BEVERLY AT THE SAME TIME I DID & I'm not sure if it really was him but he looked like it & I didn't believe you could actually get stuffed in lockers until I saw it in real life he was small & walked on tiptoe & didn't comb his wild hair full of lint or match his sagging socks & two football players had a great time putting him in his locker after taking his lunch & all the money in his pockets & making him keep the empty pockets outside of his pants the lockers were tall & he had plenty of headroom when I got him out his face streaked with dirty tears & enormous glasses askew I asked if he was okay he said just leave me alone & snatched the Kleenex from my hand as he tiptoe-ran away

I was nine or ten when I met Minister Louis Farrakhan at Mosque No. 27 on Crenshaw everyone kept saying how he wouldn't be giving that many appearances anymore because he had cancer & I stood in line with my mother & sister to meet him we had on our white MGT-GCC uniforms my mother was a captain so she had a fez & my sister & I had pristine head scarves the same thick material as our dresses & starched to perfection the line was really long but we were close to the front so my white patent leather shoes hadn't yet started to pinch when I climbed the steps of the dais & he held both his hands out for my hands & smiled & his skin was so clear I remember how shiny it was not in a greasy way but a bright kind & he called me little sister & asked my name & said it was the same as his wife's & he expected me to live up to its greatness

My dad said he took us to see both Nelson Mandela & Muhammad Ali at different times in our childhood but I don't remember either maybe we sat way in the back or something he had to be telling the truth because he taught us to read using black history flash cards & one of my favorite outfits then consisted of pink corduroy stirrup pants with a matching checked shirt & low-slung purple belt with a silver buckle plus black karate shoes & Oh God there are pictures

SPEAKING OF THOSE PICTURES in one of them with that outfit on I posed
with my sister & a giant-sized Megatron at Universal Studios I never felt
happier in my nine years of life than at that moment but only because they
didn't have Optimus Prime &(yes robots count as famous men especially
Optimus Prime)& oh the indelible grief when he died in that cartoon movie
my sister & I sat in the middle of the theater & cried way past the credits &
the ushers had to kick us out

SINCE OPTIMUS PRIME COUNTS SO DOES THE KITT CAR that same day at Universal Studios we got right in the front seat which I'm pretty sure was hard & plastic but we didn't care *Knight Rider* was our favorite show besides *CHiPS* I don't remember if we actually controlled the buttons in the car or not but we thought we did KITT had many wisecracks & what does it mean that the only famous men I remember from that day were a life-sized statue of a cartoon character & a talking car I think it means I was ahead of my time & can blame my parents for the outfit although my mother didn't like us watching too much TV one night she even pushed it with her thighs right out the front door & down the porch steps my older sisters brought it back in but it wasn't the same the screen stayed tilted to the right & for the record I didn't like David Hasselhoff too hairy but would like to confirm I did feel something like love for that car

JOSH DUHAMEL WALKED PAST ME REALLY FAST on the set of *Las Vegas* that show was always busy & us extras could always count on overtime but it wasn't a good gig to accept when you wanted to do homework between takes I had on a purple jersey midi skirt & purple silk crop top with sequins & a sheer scarf hem that fell to my waist & spaghetti straps no bra & silver stiletto sandals with ankle ties anyway Josh Duhamel was really tall & his hair dark & immobile I remember that day so well because I got sick off of the catering I couldn't eat the pork chops because I don't eat pork so I tried the calamari & the chow line was really long & they were set up outside so the food didn't stay at the right temperature & I ended up in the bathroom on set later washing my hands & face in the fancy marble sink inlaid with gold after throwing up & I didn't do that show again for a really long time & even then I brought my own smoked turkey sandwich & Sun Chips

AL PACINO IS ON THE SHORT SIDE BUT VERY GRACIOUS my sister & I were extras on the set of *Heat* & the AD seated us at the table next to where the action was taking place & he said hello to all of us & made small talk until it was time to start filming I had skinny braids that went to my waist & wardrobe put me in a pink sequined A-line swing dress with gold heels & the director asked if I could sing I said no but my sister can I'll get her but she'd left to go smoke something in a hallway or outside with another extra & I couldn't find her in time when I got back to set another woman had already taken the stage I told my sister later & she didn't even care I think mostly she was bummed that we didn't get to meet Robert DeNiro

WHEN WE MET TUPAC WE HAD JUST LEFT THE ARENA ON SUNSET BECAUSE IT WAS GAY NIGHT & WE COULDN'T GET IN we were five of us crammed into Kelly's red hatchback about to just get some Taco Bell & go home when we saw him in a black Mercedes equally crammed & we screamed & yelled We Love You! & he & his friends invited us to a hotel party which seemed sketchy to me but it was Tupac & it was Kelly's car & she wanted to go so we went it was not far away also on Sunset by the time we got a parking space a bunch of girls were already there talking to him he was surrounded & shorter than all of them his head looked like it was bigger than his body but he had really white perfect teeth & a leather vest with no shirt & all those hot tattoos we asked one of the bodyguard guys where the bathroom was so we could freshen up & of course we all had to go together & Kelly started talking about how much she wanted to get at Tupac she was from Louisiana & lived in a house in the Hollywood Hills the richest of us which was easy actually because we were mostly poor & lived in apartments but she said she wanted to get to his room & have sex with him & say he raped her can you believe that shit she wanted the money & we all laughed at first but this chick was serious we told her we weren't going for it she said whatever I'm cuter than all y'all & I drove I'ma do whatever the fuck I want she unbuttoned her top down to the lace of her white bra & walked out of the bathroom I had on one of my least favorite outfits because it was time to do the laundry I might be blocking it from memory but I think it was brown or olive green or something yuck & the four of us debated what to do about Kelly so I decided to call my dad for a ride home came out of the bathroom & asked where the pay phone was back then we all had pagers but no cell & one of the bodyguards was blocking another girl from entering the lobby she was at least 6 feet tall & barely dressed but super young in the face he asked for

genuinely not right

ID & it was a middle school ID she was only 13 he told her go home right now little girl where are your parents we were in shock but glad he seemed decent we felt like we had to tell him what Kelly was doing & she saw us coming up to him & got pissed she walked away from where she was waiting to talk to Tupac yes there were that many chicks up in there all lined up & she said let's just go & in the car she called us a bunch of lame virgins but we didn't care I said she was a skank for trying to do that & she wanted me out of her car but nobody would let her do that either we never really hung out again after that oh well I didn't really like her that much anyway when we met it was because she said I tried to steal her boyfriend but I didn't he came on to me he was the captain of the basketball team & I didn't even know he was a basketball player at all I was just trying to study for my SATs & that is a whole other story

WALTER MOSLEY MOSTLY LOOKED AT OUR CLEAVAGE I was with three friends at AWP & didn't think that was appropriate at writing functions I was so green a grad student & probably shouldn't be saying this now but for whatever reason he felt comfortable enough to lower his eyes slowly chestward then raise them & say you have to write every single day

creepy

THE WAYANS BROTHERS DID NOT LOOK AT ALL (neither did Bell Biv DeVoe for that matter which I can't stand them anyway because boys in my junior high school used to sing that stupid That Girl is Poison lyric to me all the time until I clothes-lined Imani when he grabbed my ass in P.E.) I was with my friends at the Beverly Center again in a velvet choker & something from Wet Seal & just out of high school & not stealing stuff from the Hello Kitty store anymore & we were not light enough or tall enough I don't think & they are from New York *makes sense now all of this has happened*

I AM FROM LOS ANGELES OBVIOUSLY & the first famous man I saw was Eddie Murphy we were on Slauson it was dark early because of winter & we got off the bus with my mother we had just seen *Beverly Hills Cop* a few weeks before & I looked into the junky brown car at the stoplight & said Mama. That. Is. Eddie. Murphy! & I pointed my sister said that IS him! & she pointed we had on matching purple & pink coats from Montgomery Ward's I could tell he mouthed to the passenger I think they recognize me & he laughed a real Eddie Murphy laugh we could see all his teeth & he beeped the horn & we all waved as he drove off & I wondered why the hell he was in that junky car with a guy in a striped tracksuit I think I was 8

COMEDIANS CAN BE THE BEST 20 years ago I sat in the front row at this comedy spot off Fairfax with my sister when Chris Tucker first came to L.A. he was skinny & young & I wanted to stop laughing during his set because I had done like 100 crunches that day but I couldn't it hurt but I just couldn't we had dinner there too & my sister had three hot wings left & he said I'm hungry dammit! & looked at her food & looked at her & said Gimme that chicken you ain't gon eat that chicken & she passed him the plate & he ate it right there at the microphone This is some good ass chicken he said & this other comedian stopped us on the way out he wasn't anywhere near as funny as Chris Tucker but whatever he was sort of charming gave me his card & said there was a party the next day he wrote down the address I went with a friend when we got there there was no party just him & a huge guy who seemed sheisty & my friend was like nope but I had to use the bathroom & we had driven all the way to the Valley in my Sentra & he was a comedian wtf was he gonna do so we had to go in he tried to give us drinks but I didn't drink back then & when I came out of the bathroom he pressed me to the wall & tried to kiss me & feel me up but I was a head taller than he was in my white platform shoes yes white platform sandals & drawstring linen pants & he played with the string I said oh! I left something in the car that I brought for you & my friend was already outside smoking a beedi & we got the f out & back on the 101 & wouldn't you know it a few months later Chris Tucker & Faizon Love came to Musicland where I worked & pretended to buy a polka tape he made me ring it up & everything which got on my nerves because I had to void the ticket he said what the hell would I look like bumping polka & the way he was looking at me like I was a plate of chicken & got too close & asked if I had a boyfriend which I did actually that boyfriend would rape me later that week right behind my apartment in an old Toyota Corona & wearing his Crenshaw High School letter jacket he was the quarterback neighborhood famous oh well it's the end of 1993 anyway & Chris Tucker kind of made me nervous at the same time I was trying not to laugh

EDWARD NORTON JUST STARED he was on his cell phone going up the escalator at Port Authority I was going down & when we met in the middle he said you are gorgeous I was 36 & so NYC in a black turtleneck & salt-and-pepper curls & just starting not to be sad or afraid

PRINCE CALLED ME UP ONSTAGE AT THE PONTIAC SILVERDOME & my scary ass didn't go up there my sisters waited in line for hours so we could get good tickets & we lucked up on the 8th row & used the light bill money to pay for it I mean who needs lights when you got Prince & the day before the concert I bought a supertight electric blue column dress from Charlotte Russe at the Livonia Mall it had a back-of-the-knee-high slit I was 21 & we all screamed when *The Beautiful Ones* started up & I began to cry even though he didn't play any of the old hits straight but because everything was spectacular I didn't sit in my seat the whole time & was losing my voice & then a burly guy with a headset motioned that I should go with him & come on stage & WHAT I froze I mean WHAT I knew that dress did not make me look shy but I thought if I went up there I would faint & I'm not the best dancer I thought I'd probably cry like an idiot & then pass out & wake up & pass out again so I said no & shook my head no my heart beating fast & sweating my dress into a darker blue

meme

WHEN I MET ANDRE 3000 AT THE RALPH'S IN BURBANK at 2 am after
my 27th birthday party I had on a black leather coat with a real fox fur collar
sorry & just got my first streak of gray hair in the front he really liked that &
I asked if I could take a picture with him I thought I was hot shit in my pale
pink silk wrap dress & black stilettos so I walked off but really I'd had too
much champagne & had fallen in love with an indifferent man &(missed an
opportunity to be nicer)

I MET KEYSHAWN JOHNSON ON THE USC CAMPUS IN ONE OF THE DORM REC ROOMS it was low lit & he was playing pool the friend I was with pointed him out & he nodded at us & shook hands I had on a green denim knee-length FUBU jacket & black bodysuit with my sister's dark green men's Levis for the low rise waist before they made those for women & fake black Timbs I don't remember why I was there but wherever my friend invited me I always tried to go we were just hanging out probably he was in his second or third year at SC & I think that was the night he felt me up & I did like & want him but not like that I wanted something more like love we had known each other since middle school but didn't talk for a while after that although eventually we did become friends again & so much happened between us I could write a book about it but I've lost interest in pain

ALLEN IVERSON USED TO HANG OUT AT A NIGHTCLUB IN VIRGINIA BEACH WHEN I WAS STATIONED IN NORFOLK & all the so-called gold digger types came out to see & be seen but I didn't know that until we were already there I went with a girlfriend from Brooklyn & she had on short shorts & a crop top & platform sandals & I wore stilettos & a satiny black column dress floor length & slinky with cut outs at the midriff & thigh-high side slits & criss-cross tie straps in the back I was in the best shape of my life & had to leave the ship with a sweatshirt on because that dress was completely unsat & could've gotten me in trouble & maybe I had on underwear maybe I didn't but I knew I felt powerful & in the mood to reject all advances & since my boyfriend bought me the dress & I knew he would meet us later I felt pretty safe & for a while no one in the crowd noticed us dancing my friend professional winding & me doing the L.A. two-step then this strange but semi-cute dude came up to me & insisted on buying me a drink & staring at my figure instead of my face & saying over & over that if he was my boyfriend he wouldn't have let me go out looking like I was looking & I should let him trade places with the chump & the chump aka my actual boyfriend couldn't hear but he could see & it seemed like he liked being envied all posted up in the back of the club with the other West Indian dudes drinking Guinness & waiting for dancehall remixes but when the guy tried to put his hand on my naked waist & whisper in my ear all of a sudden there he was with his muscle man squad pulling me close & we left in time to see Allen Iverson in his cornrows & oversized jersey & jean shorts & clean Nikes get into the driver's side of a white Bentley overcrowded with half-drunk half-dressed girls

MY TWO OLDER SISTERS MET DANNY GLOVER OFF RODEO & LA BREA
BACK IN THE MID-1980S they had underage partied the night before & still
high on weed & drinking Mad Dog 20/20 & not even from paper bags in
broad daylight & their hair a mess when he rolled up to them in a midnight
blue Mercedes & said y'all are too young & too beautiful to be walking down
the street drinking that garbage like alcoholics in the afternoon & you better
promise you won't do it again & they promised & tossed the bottles into the
nearest trash bin they both had on ironed Levis 501s & ruffle-sleeved blouses
& white Nikes & kept future walks liquor-free & made sure to keep their hair
done too because you never know who might see you

TERRELL OWENS PRIVATE MESSAGED ME ON MYSPACE I didn't believe
it was actually him but he insisted & said I had a nice smile I returned the
compliment that was way back when his career was promising & his body fat
must have been at zero &(when I said how cool it was that our sons have the
same name I didn't get anymore all caps messages)

THESE DAYS I DON'T MEET ANY CELEBRITIES AT ALL but I did go on a date with a former pro football player right when I felt ready for another relationship something simple but not precluding depth & he was very sweet & straightforward which was good but then he said he didn't like to read & his text messages were a little off i.e. *did you know God sometimes makes matches while we still up in heaven? I heard that from a grapevine* so although his body was a wall of muscle & he spoke kindly to the waitress at dinner & complimented my 4-inch heels & black skinny jeans & said he wanted to learn a lot from me I saw too much work & I already have a job & a kid so told him I wanted to move slowly & neither of us called the other back again

A GUY I CHATTED WITH ONLINE TRIED TO IMPRESS ME & EVERY OTHER WOMAN WITH HIS SELFIES WITH USHER & various other celebs I couldn't name because I don't watch sports or nearly as much television as I used to & he also called me cutie I am 40 years old he called me girl & my patience for such thoughtlessness has fully waned & the exchange makes me realize my definition of seduction has all the way changed & makes me wonder how long I have to wait for the world to change too & makes me think my fragility my accumulated ailments mean I'll just have to miss out on certain things & because I have to stay home a lot to heal maybe I might not ever meet my match especially not one who thinks before he speaks & he said I did three video shoots this weekend what did you do & I said I signed the contract for my fifth book & working on a PhD application he said doing the most I see & I see too

A MAN I MET ON TINDER TOOK ME TO SEE LIONEL RICHIE AT RED
ROCKS AMPHITHEATER I had on 3-inch gold heels stupidly because you
have to climb approximately 8 million steps which slope at a 45 degree angle
but redeemed myself by keeping a pair of flats in the car also gold luckily
matching my black slacks & ecru shell & light sweater I was glad I brought
the sweater even though it was June since when the sun went down it still
wasn't warm enough & my date also let me wear his jacket & wrapped an
arm around my shoulders & we had just met but it wasn't weird at all just a
moment that made me love dating in my late 30s & our whole row sang along
to all the songs & on that outdoor screen Lionel Richie looked like he hadn't
aged a day since 1988

AT THE END OF SUMMER I MET A GUY WHO LOOKED LIKE A SIX-FOOT-TWO LENNY KRAVITZ BUT HE TURNED OUT TO BE ANOTHER NARCISSISTIC SOCIOPATH & where is the law against men that fine & that crazy but at least I could tell within the first 30 minutes of conversation which included tales of his multiple cars & failed pro football career & travels to China where he had adventures with sex traffickers & drug dealers & later (because I had to finish my raspberry cheesecake & glass of rosé) the breakup with his Chinese baby's mother who he called his former weed bitch & his switch from Christianity to Judaism because he said he wanted to be rich & what in the world happened to this man to make him think it's okay to reveal all of that to a stranger what kind of man does that I thought but it's the kind who makes sure you arrive at the restaurant in time to see him speed into the parking lot in a black on black Porsche & the kind who wears not one but three diamond rings not one but three gold chains & after he hugs you hello reaches back into the car to grab his Louis Vuitton man purse & the zing of attraction crackles to ash because when I met him at the bookstore he claimed to be a small-time restaurateur he had on jeans & Frye boots & a worn Jimi Hendrix T-shirt no gold no chains just a leather cuff & a zillion tattoos & his arms were CUT so when he asked to buy me a drink later I gave him my number I had on zero makeup my 20 post-surgical pounds & an orange & white maxi tank dress & raffia wedges & I should have known better because he was 10 years younger & chose one of those self-published looking wealth management books & wandered to the money-oriented magazine aisle but his attention made me feel lovely at a time when I needed to feel lovely but I'll be damned if I get dumb so I blocked him & changed his name to Red Flags & avoid making eye contact with men at the Barnes & Noble

MY BEST FRIEND FROM JUNIOR HIGH SCHOOL LOOKS A LOT LIKE DJIMON HONSOU & he still loves me & I will love him forever but we totally messed it up I had not yet dealt with my issues & he had not yet dealt with his issues & we both were with other people in our late 20s so when he kissed me after a baseball game I played barefoot in because I'd worn four-inch wedge sandals with bell bottom jeans & a crochet-style crop top I didn't really want to stop him & he said the earth moved & I didn't roll my eyes & my son was in the car eating M&Ms & smiling at us & he was only three & won't remember but I'll never forget I thought faux Djimon would break up with his girlfriend like I was ready to shut down the thing I had just started with a Nigerian guy but he said can I have some time & instead of saying hasn't it been long enough & or how about no & because I thought he was my friend I said sure but after a year then two then three of back & forth I quit I quit & dated a painter who worked in oil & had some gorgeous pieces in the Smithsonian but the way he kissed felt more cold fish than genius strokes & maybe it was me maaaaaybe & after some drama & some therapy & seeing him again a decade later & making out again & saying no to the undefined because you can't rush a Pisces into making a decision I am tough enough to know what I can take & satisfied with keeping stars on the screen & out of my eyes my well-used heart

WATCHING KOOL MOE DEE ON *UNSUNG* MAKES ME THINK ABOUT CELIBACY I mean he never married or had children & although one friend says he has women on rotation another calls him the monk MC but I just think he's an introvert & maybe scarred by his father stabbing his mother a hell of a thing to witness at 12 & it makes me wonder if being alone isn't easier but a braver choice to be at peace with your own expectations rather than those of others & it made me wonder if another year free of men might turn into five or ten or the rest of my life like my mother who feels perfectly content spending her time not cooking any man's food or washing his underwear & made me wonder if I could do more or less with my life if I had a man in it or if my son is missing out on more than he should & it made me wonder if I am enough but only for a minute because I realized I like my body unassailed by tenderness or roughness & free of obligation I like my peace & I tried to make my teenager watch the video for "Wild, Wild West" on YouTube he gave it 30 seconds pressed pause & backed out of the room I probably should have played "How Ya Like Me Now"

WHEN I SAW OCHOCINCO I HAD TO THINK ABOUT ALL OF THE WAYS I HAD BEEN FAKE or lied about my feelings or calculated a response & why risk dismissal of a real self when you can create a façade one easily taken down & reconstructed why let people into your real house with its rust & clutter & unframed prints & dessicated parsley in the crisper & so what if your history of poverty is evident & you ask yourself is that who you are & who are you afraid of or is the surface attention itself your addiction & in Atlanta getting a buffet dinner at Eats making sure Ochocinco who is famous for both playing football & head-butting his fiancé when she allegedly caught him cheating making sure he doesn't touch you when he reaches a little too close when you are both getting silverware & your armor is a burgundy vegan leather tank top with peplum hem & a black midi skirt & low-heel slightly-over-the-knee leather boots & you can feel the men in the restaurant looking as you walk by but they don't speak & you practice what you've learned you walk tall walk pageant straight & manage to eat greens & cornbread with whatever kind of grown woman grace

BILL CLINTON IS A STELLAR SPEAKER BUT KEITH RICHARDS MEH it was hard to look at his tobacco paper face & skeletal physical reality & stringy white headband to match his evening coat but I remember his kindness to fans & Bill Clinton seemed to really like him a lot apparently they had been vacation home neighbors I didn't meet either of them but only because I was not that big a fan of either to be geeking out like a few others at the gala who were of that generation all eye shine & moist grins & asking for selfie permission when I took a cab back home later it occurred to me in the Lincoln Tunnel that the guy who invited me expected something since he tried to linger in the goodbye hug but hell to the no no way & after that he didn't send any more gold-engraved pens or leather-bound journals in the mail I had on a strapless dress white taffeta bodice with an asymmetrical peplum hem & black chiffon skirt I had to Cinderella-lift when I walked so it wouldn't drag the floor

THE DAY DAVID BOWIE DIED I LEARNED THAT 40 YEARS AGO IT SEEMS HE DEFLOWERED A TEENAGER & it's all over the internet I mean Ziggy Stardust the Goblin King Starman for the love of _____ got a virgin high & laid her across a hotel bed & entered her body with his body & so the f what about the 1970s & his red & yellow kimono he brought underage girls into his hotel room & gave them hash & had a threesome what a wild time huh what a moonage what a daydream & in the Thrillist article I read the girl now woman says the universe was looking out for her she said it was beautiful she said she was special she said she regrets nothing she said who wouldn't want to lose their virginity to Bowie but somehow not long after he had his way she's kidnapped by Jimmy Page & sequestered in a hotel for years until cheated on & dumped & finds herself at a Bel-Air party on Quaaludes in a white dress & bleeding from her nose

MY SISTER MET HUGH HEFNER AT A SUSHI BAR CALLED GEISHA HOUSE IN HOLLYWOOD he definitely had on a purple crushed velvet jacket & my sister said he was surrounded by some "nasty-looking girls" & he smooth came up with hey honey & smiled & she made the untranslatable sound that is the Black people version of ew & ugh is inadequate she was like what is he even looking at she had on a black crop top that was basically a bra with spaghetti straps & macramé & hip-length fringe covering her midriff & she just wanted to get some California rolls with her white friends so they kept on walking

WHEN I WAS IN MY EARLY 30S I SAW ELTON JOHN IN A NIGHTCLUB IN ATLANTA CALLED TONGUE & GROOVE my sister thought he was an imposter but his haircut seemed right & no one could miss those rhinestone or maybe diamond-framed eyeglasses & lime green paisley suit purple satin shirt & matching necktie except maybe the drunk twentysomethings dancing slash stumbling you could smell the alcohol in the humid air & feel the spills fuse to your shoe soles & I was unlucky I had just gotten dumped & some fool splashed half a Long Island Iced Tea on my white sheath dress & I was ready to go & dancing was supposed to make me feel better but instead marked the end of seeing nightclubs as fun despite the wake of Elton John whizzing by so close I could see the fabulous gap in his teeth

I HAVEN'T MET JOSÉ JAMES YET BUT I'VE COME REALLY CLOSE at concerts in New York with Ashaki who flew in from L.A. & in Denver where I sat behind Dianne Reeves with my date I loved the new music especially *U R the 1* because of the backbeat but I knew I wouldn't try to say anything to him afterward since I didn't want to be rude to my date a cute half-Irish half-Mexican ginger whose name was James ironically & my second choice since my actual date got held up in a work meeting across town but I didn't want to go alone & embarrassingly James could only afford the tip when the check came & worse he approached the band members smoking outside after the set & gave them his bootleg VistaPrint business card I kept walking to my car when he started bragging about how he knew people who could help them a band that had just gotten back from a European tour to find a nice venue in Denver & never mind they were already playing in a legendary one in my mortified head I said stop James please stop but he didn't get my psychic transmission I dropped him off & never saw him again but I didn't want to go home so I met the first choice guy for drinks at a dive bar & he beat me at air hockey it was fun I had on a white pencil skirt with a black camisole & wide black leather belt & that outfit got a lot of likes on Instagram

I FOLLOW THE ROCK ON INSTAGRAM & one of these days I'm going to meet him & get a muscle hug & find some way to yell FOCUS! like he does when he's working out & really I don't care if that sounds lame I just hope I'm not having a bad hair day & have on something photo-ready like my pink wrap dress & suede wedges that make me look 5'10" & I hope it'll be at a good time for him so I don't feel guilty about what my son calls fan-girling & clearly someone who watches *Scorpion King* twice a year on silent & sees every new release on opening weekend is committed but really I've been a fan since my roommate in the Navy had a WWE poster of him above her bed & got me watching wrestling again way back in the late '90s & his trash talk & independent eyebrow inspired me to boss up & get through dealing with the monumental bullshit women in general & women in the military have to slog through between unwanted advances & wardrobe policing & femininity policing & language policing & lack of intellectual trust like the time I said yessamassa I'se a-sorry massa please don't beat me massa with a real non-yessamassa tone & face when my two supervisors tried to bully me into apologizing for something I didn't do but I stood my own ground in my uniform & combat boots & Toni Braxton haircut my neck & shoulders on swoll from lifting anyway how many times will the average person get to meet The Rock I only need to meet him once I promise

I saw Q-Tip at The Original Pancake House in Fort Lee it was a sunny day in New Jersey pre-Hurricane Sandy & he walked in with a white girl dressed in pink Uggs & a matching velour Juicy tracksuit & he breezed past our table in his brown leather jacket & clean Cortez sneaks like he was on a mission leaving her to trail behind & it's funny what one's first instinct is to wonder but nevermind that he had immaculate skin & is way taller than I thought & hella fine so I don't even remember what I wore that day I mean shit

I WENT TO A FANCY STEAKHOUSE & MY CLASS WAS SHOWING by that I mean working class by that I mean I had worked a lot of overtime & wanted to treat myself but I couldn't help thinking of Martin Lawrence when he said on his TV show "I like my women classy, not showing all the assy" when I got there because for a supposedly classy bunch at the steakhouse I saw a whole lot of assy I mean y'all it was a lot of T&A & it shocked me a little that so many women over 60 could or would wear skintight sequined mini dresses & 5-inch heels & grind on their toupeed or grayed men grooving with their paunches on an outdoor dance floor while a cover band played "This is How We Do It" & some of them were really drunk & I thought wow is this what I looked like when I was in my 20s ridiculous & stuffed into discomfort & I can't believe I believed in it & what does that say about me & what does it mean when a woman past retirement age in a red Léger & Louboutins stumbles past me her platinum-encrusted hand shaking before her martini glass slipped & shattered on her squeak & her companion around the same age with a gentle white fro kind of fell into our table & couldn't stop himself the busboy cleaning up the drink had to hold him upright at the same time & when I saw all of that I felt a lot of emotion I felt uncomfortable I felt confused I felt like I was at a human circus but isn't it all & still I thought how sad how terrible & how strange a culture that this is what fun looks like to some people but I admit I had a kind of fun people watching & the food was divine & the band played Prince which made me both happy & sad & not like dancing & I came home with leftover orange tamarind salmon & garlic mashed potatoes & a little of the sliced squash but not the apple cake & maybe yes I felt out of place with my TJ Maxx outfit I had on a loose silk top that fell past my hips neon pink with a triple-layered hem & split back with ripped jeans & my shoes unremarkable 1″ tan leather wedges since I can't wear heels anymore & was I being a hater I thought to myself what if I could would I & would that be me in 20 years if I could still stuff myself into discomfort & variously pretend so petty or not petty it felt like I had been through present & past or heaven & hell at once then back to earth which is home in my sweats making my son a grilled cheese & cracking jokes with a lingering sidecar wit & I didn't see any celebs that night that night the stars didn't know who they were or they did & both fought against the dying & rushed toward it & you could call this angsty navel-gazing or midlife crisis or instead a clarity of observation

WHO DID I SEE AT THE BOOKSTORE IN THE MINNEAPOLIS AIRPORT
BUT SAMUEL L. JACKSON IN A GRAY SWEATSUIT & I had on my gained-
10-pounds-muffin top jeans it was mostly empty in there I was buying books
for my son & baby nephew I almost didn't say anything but he walked right
by me I couldn't not whisper *Sam Jackson?* with my eyes narrowed & he is
kind of tall he said And you are? I just gave him my first name he said Oh
Khadijah! with a wide genuine smile & an exclamation point so of course I
got nervous I didn't want him to think I was a groupie I'm kind of paranoid
like that but that's stupid I had on old jeans & my hair was a mess & hello
muffin top but I managed to say *big fan nice to meet you* & shake his hand &
walk to my gate & when I called my mother she said you should have given
him a *Black Peculiar*!

So when a Famous Poet decides he wants to call me I don't really want to talk very long & I don't believe his flattering emails I mean I heard he was enamored but I also knew the long list of ex-girlfriends & I also had to iron my son's clothes for school & help him with his homework so I said I am not interested in being an ingénue & we laughed & he would call & say May I speak to the ingénue & I was busy I work long hours & go to the doctor a lot & barely have time to write & hardly ever draw anymore & I couldn't take him seriously not really I mean I can't really help what I look like but I can help what *it* looks like so it took months after he sat in the front row at the Center for Book Arts & nodded at my poems for him to tell me that he could see the small of my back because he was sitting behind me & he remembered I had on an eggshell blouse with a high collar & pearl buttons & it took months before I went to the Harlem Arts Salon for his book release party & after it was over he walked my son & I to the elevator & squeezed my hair no one had ever really squeezed my hair so the next day I replied to his email I said I would be in the City I had on suede knee boots & a trench because it was fall & we ended up walking somewhere in Manhattan after Thai food holding hands & a random guy telling him You Doing it Big! & a few months later he would push me into a hotel closet at a writing conference & grab my breasts so hard it hurt & saying I liked it until I screamed as loud as I could in his face when he wouldn't stop & why couldn't all this only be about name-dropping & brand names & puddintang ask me again I'll tell you the same

WHEN I SAW JOHN SINGLETON BUYING A BEAN PIE AT SIMPLY WHOLESOME I KNEW I HAD DONE THE RIGHT THING cutting off all lovers & ex-lovers all man candy & even decent prospects & coming to L.A. for my 40th birthday to hang out with my best friends & also who doesn't love bean pie if they've had some bean pie & my son came with me his face all smiles because spicy Jamaican patty & cream soda heaven & even the live music at Simply is perfect & even though I'd had two surgeries & my newly cut up gut prone to protest I was alive in my hometown & seeing celebs just like old times & when I was young I could in equal measure celebrate & take everything about living for granted but 40 is so cool 40 is seeing & knowing not seeing & wanting 40 holds beauty as the accumulation of bliss & survival 40 widens its arms 40 seeks all the June sun instead of shade & flies with more than usual mechanical luster & says yes to all the right things 40 knows what it wants & mostly gets its every fineness

ANY OTHER NAME: A POSTSCRIPT

Khadijah means wife of the prophet. Nothing about my name is casual. Your mouth has to make an effort. You have to commit to all eight letters, all three syllables, no nickname. It means something Uber drivers, the Muslim ones, all men, want to tell me about even after I say yes when they ask do I know. They want to know how old I am and where I'm from they want to get in my business

where is my husband. Some men can't stop telling me who I am or what exactly is so incredible about me or what they had to take or offer without asking. They still say it's my fault I am beautiful. I was raised as a Muslim. *In the name of Allah Most Gracious Most Merciful* shouldn't I thank God for the kind of beauty that makes me so desirable an object so in demand by strangers you might say my name cursed me to solitude. I don't see any prophets around, do you? If so, pass out my number tell him I said what's up where have you been all my life. I know it's a line but people like familiar things like fellow boring straight people hey

I'll be 44 in a few years and I have a tradition to live up to a prophecy perhaps. Chop chop. I cut off my hair because I wanted to begin again with something on my body no man has touched. I wanted to press rewind. I still want the kind of purity that cures men of acculturated entitlement. I want a little silence when I walk down the street or get into the back seat of a hired car in any city I travel to. Maybe I have to marry myself. Maybe I am my own prophet. I want to stop reacting and keep creating and to do that maybe I need a new kind of hijab that makes me safer unseen, free of both sound and adornment. I could use that kind of safety.

Sartre said hell is other people and by the token of time through the ages, surely a French philosopher knows whether man equals less than desire and *surely man is in loss, except those who do good works, and enjoin one another to the truth, and enjoin one another to patience and constancy.* My mother told me I should keep some things to myself. She should have said keep yourself to yourself but it was in her nature to be generous. I learned that kind of giving leads to further taking and it's a light that attracts parasites. What's an ex-Muslim girl to do

keep praying. The world of prophets is elite. They don't just let anyone in, lol not wives and sometimes I want to cut myself out of all possible institutional pictures. Sometimes I am in a collage I made myself and I have a new name. I have a name I have given myself and I'm the only one who knows what it means. But that doesn't make sense *Bismillah ar-rahman ar-rahim* like the first time I was taken from myself my father asked me what I learned and that is what I learned. I learned I had no father but I could walk in the rain and let my hair rise up in the night become a black halo *aaameeeeeeeeeeen* curling closer to my head as if to love it,

softly greeting as if saying peace be unto me. A man can break you with your own love if you don't remember who you are among the nonbelievers. All praises due to the part of me that listens to herself first. The first time I drew a rose I couldn't stop layering in new petals. My small right hand filled the flimsy newsprint with red Crayola spirals, the lines unbroken, the endless making as sweet as being out of the order other people like to think you are born to.

ACKNOWLEDGMENTS

For publishing parts of this work, sometimes in different iterations, my deepest gratitude to the editors at Argos Books, *Aster(ix) Journal*, *Barrelhouse*, *Bettering American Poetry*, *Brooklyn Magazine*, *Buzzfeed*, *DIAGRAM*, *elsewhere*, *Fence*, *Feminist Wire*, *Gulf Coast*, *Hyperallergic*, *Poor Claudia*, *Rhino*, *Spoon River Review*, *The Offing*, *The Rumpus*, and to the editors at Sibling Rivalry Press, who published 16 of these pieces as a digital chapbook in November 2013.

For their advice, encouragement, love, support and attention, always: my mother, Denelda; Dr. Ashaki M. Jackson, Dr. Bettina Judd, ariel robello, and Tiffany Anderson; Kim Smith, Taliah Goedar, Vanessa White. A special thanks to Terrance Hayes for his critical eye; an extra special thanks to my son for eating leftovers, frozen dinners and a lot of cereal while I wrote; the Front Range poetry community for listening to and encouraging these poems as they began; L'Erin Asantewaa, for the reminders; Arielle Greenberg; KMA Sullivan, Phillip Williams and YesYes Books; and last but not least, The Grind daily writing group, for their dedication.

KHADIJAH QUEEN is the author of *Conduit* (Black Goat / Akashic Books 2008), *Black Peculiar* (Noemi Press 2011), which won the Noemi book award for poetry and was a finalist for the Gatewood Prize at Switchback Books; *Fearful Beloved* (Argos Books 2015), a hybrid collection framed by a letter to fear written during artist Ann Hamilton's Park Avenue Armory installation the event of a thread; and the narrative collection *I'm So Fine: A List of Famous Men & What I Had On* (YesYes Books 2017). She is also the author of *Non-Sequitur* (Litmus Press 2015), a verse play which won the Leslie Scalapino Award for Innovative Women Performance Writers. The prize included a full production staged in New York City at Theaterlab from December 10 – 20, 2015 by The Relationship theater company. Individual works appear in *Fence, Tin House, Gulf Coast, The Offing, jubilat, Tupelo Quarterly, Poor Claudia, Best American Nonrequired Reading, The Volta Book of Poets, Fire & Ink: A Social Action Anthology, The Force of What's Possible* and widely in other journals and anthologies. She serves as core faculty in poetry and playwriting for the low-residency Mile-High MFA in creative writing at Regis University. She is also raising a teenager.

ALSO FROM YESYES BOOKS

FULL-LENGTH COLLECTIONS

i be, but i ain't by Aziza Barnes
The Feeder by Jennifer Jackson Berry
Love the Stranger by Jay Deshpande
Blues Triumphant by Jonterri Gadson
North of Order by Nicholas Gulig
Meet Me Here at Dawn by Sophie Klahr
I Don't Mind If You're Feeling Alone by Thomas Patrick Levy
If I Should Say I Have Hope by Lynn Melnick
some planet by jamie mortara
Boyishly by Tanya Olson
Pelican by Emily O'Neill
The Youngest Butcher in Illinois by Robert Ostrom
A New Language for Falling Out of Love by Meghan Privitello
American Barricade by Danniel Schoonebeek
The Anatomist by Taryn Schwilling
Gilt by Raena Shirali
Panic Attack, USA by Nate Slawson
[insert] boy by Danez Smith
Man vs Sky by Corey Zeller
The Bones of Us by J. Bradley
    [*Art by Adam Scott Mazer*]

CHAPBOOK COLLECTIONS

VINYL 45S

After by Fatimah Asghar
Dream with a Glass Chamber by Aricka Foreman
Pepper Girl by Jonterri Gadson
Bad Star by Rebecca Hazelton
Inside My Electric City by Caylin Capra-Thomas
Makeshift Cathedral by Peter LaBerge
Still, the Shore by Keith Leonard
Please Don't Leave Me Scarlett Johansson by Thomas Patrick Levy
Juned by Jenn Marie Nunes
A History of Flamboyance by Justin Phillip Reed
No by Ocean Vuong

BLUE NOTE EDITIONS

Beastgirl & Other Origin Myths by Elizabeth Acevedo

COMPANION SERIES

Inadequate Grave by Brandon Courtney
The Rest of the Body by Jay Deshpande